123 SESAME STREET®

I Want to Be... Treasury

6 Classic Stories

Dover Publications, Inc.
Mineola, New York

Copyright

Bibliographical Note

Sesame Street I Want to Be... Treasury—6 Classic Stories, first published by Dover Publications, Inc., in 2011, is a new compilation, containing the following books: *I Want to Be President,* first published by Western Publishing Company in conjunction with Children's Television Workshop, in 1993; *I Want to Be a Firefighter,* first published by Western Publishing Company in conjunction with Children's Television Workshop, in 1991; *I Want to Be a Doctor,* first published by Western Publishing Company in conjunction with Children's Television Workshop, in 1991; *I Want to Be a Ballet Dancer,* first published by Western Publishing Company in conjunction with Children's Television Workshop, in 1993; *I Want to Be a Veterinarian,* first published by Western Publishing Company in conjunction with Children's Television Workshop, in 1992; and *I Want to Be a Teacher,* first published by Western Publishing Company in conjunction with Children's Television Workshop, in 1991.

International Standard Book Number
ISBN 13: 978-0-486-33038-9
ISBN 10: 0-486-33038-9

Manufactured in the United States by Courier Corporation
33038901
www.doverpublications.com

CONTENTS

I Want to Be President 3

I Want to Be a Firefighter 27

I Want to Be a Doctor 51

I Want to Be a Ballet Dancer 75

I Want to Be a Veterinarian 99

I Want to Be a Teacher 123

★ I WANT TO BE ★
PRESIDENT

By Michaela Muntean
Illustrated by Tom Brannon

One day my mommy and I stopped to watch a big
black car go by. Everyone else stopped, too, because
it was so exciting. Police cars with flashing lights
surrounded the big car.

My mommy told me that the President was riding in the
big car! The President is the leader of the United States
of America.

That night my mommy and daddy and I watched the
President give a speech on television.

The President was speaking at the United Nations.
The United Nations is a place where people from almost
every country in the world meet to solve problems.
Giving speeches is just one of the many things the
President does. Being President is a very important job.

I think that I would be a good President when I grow up. But first I will have to be elected by the people of the United States. When I run for President, I will have posters and buttons that say: VOTE FOR BETTY LOU.

After I am elected, I will live in the White House on Pennsylvania Avenue in Washington, D.C.

I will have a special place to work called the
Oval Office. I will help pass new laws. I will help
make decisions about spending money. That's
called making a budget.

The President's job is so big that she needs helpers. The President's helpers are members of the Cabinet. Before I make a decision, I will meet with my Cabinet and listen to what everyone has to say.

Sometimes I will be in a parade. I will get to ride in a big car and wave to everyone. I think that part of the job will be fun.

Whenever I have to go somewhere, I will fly
on *Air Force One*. It is a special plane just for me,
the President.

Sometimes I will go to other countries to meet with their leaders. That is called a state visit. Some countries have a king or a queen. Others have a President like me.

I will meet with reporters from newspapers and magazines. They will ask me questions, and I will try my best to answer them. It is important to tell the people of the United States what the President is doing.

Newsworld

The President

NEWS TODAY
VIA SATELLITE
SHAQUILLE HAS THE MAGIC TOUCH
ORLANDO PACKAGE PAYS
SHAQ $3.5M, #1 ROOKIE YEAR;
DEAL MAY TOTAL $40M, 1C
MILWAUKEE GIVES
BASEBALL HONOR
BY THE NUMBERS
BREWERS TO RETIRE No. 34
FOR ROLLIE FINGERS, 1,10C
• BASEBALL REPORT, 1,4,5C

SHAQUILLE O'NEAL:
#1 Pick NBA TODAY, 1C

THE NATION'S NEWSPAPER

CLINT

Betty Lou in charge

FRI./SAT./SUN., AUG. 7-9, 1992

NEWSLINE
A QUICK READ ON THE NEWS

WALL STREET: Dow Jones industrial average falls
24.34 points to 3,352.31 as disappointing earnings taint their
luck analysts say GM needs to accelerate cost-cutting. 2B
Plus beverage research directors give their advice on
best buys now, 3B; a bullish market Dun Darlmak, 4B

• TRIAL: Four officers surrender to federal
marshals and prosecutors must prove the federal
intended to deprive Rodney King's civil rights, 3A

CONVENTION: Austin has left, and we have more of
the highlights of this weekend of
the gang gathering in the workplace
as she received a to her FBI
organization to
Washington

BusinessWorld

The Global Economy

DAILY TIMES
35¢
© 1992, The Herald News

plans for 30,000 fewer

"R estructuring the
Postal Service will
be completed within 90
days ..."
— Postmaster General

restructuring of the Postal Service will be completed within 90
days, Runyon said.
Saying the Postal Service
needs to be "more accountable,
more credible, and more com-
petitive," Runyon said the
changes will improve customer
service, service, as delaying a
postal rate increase and estab-
lishing two trial toll-free tele-

Cutting positions that
morphed positions ...
about $1 billion alone, he said.
"Competition affects our decision very much," he said ...

a rigid

ou
ak

TIMES NOW

On holidays there are special events at
the White House. At Eastertime there is an
Easter-egg hunt on the White House lawn.

At Christmastime we have an enormous tree decorated with hundreds of little lights. As the President, I will be the one who pulls the switch to turn on the lights.

Sometimes the President gives medals to heroes and heroines for bravery or good deeds. We have a special ceremony in the Rose Garden.

The President has a big job with many responsibilities, but I won't mind. I will work hard and be a good leader for my country.

When I grow up...

I want to be President!

I Want to Be
A Firefighter

By Linda Lee Maifair
Illustrated by Tom Cooke

My uncle Grady is a firefighter. Today is his
birthday. Mommy baked a cake to surprise him.
   "I will surprise Uncle Grady, too," I told my mommy.
"I, Grover, will dress up like a firefighter."

Mommy told me that firefighters wear helmets to
protect themselves when they fight fires.

I found this hat in a trunk up in the attic. It looks
like a firefighter's helmet.

Mommy said firefighters need special masks and air tanks because it is very difficult to breathe in smoky buildings.

I went to my room and put on my catcher's mask. Then I looked for something that would help me breathe in a smoky building. Aha! I found the perfect thing.

Mommy told me that firefighters use swooshing
water from big hoses to put out fires. They wear
rubber raincoats and tall rubber boots to keep dry.
Oh, look! Here is my old slicker. It still fits me.
And Grandpa's fishing boots are very tall!

I could not wait for Uncle Grady to see me, Grover, in a firefighter's outfit. I ran to answer the door.

"Surprise!" we both said at the same time. Uncle Grady was wearing his firefighter's outfit, too! He wore it just for me. He calls it his turnout gear.

"Grover," he said, "you look like a real firefighter!
Would you like to go with me to the firehouse?"
"Oh, yes, please," I said.

When we got there, nobody was home. "Oh, my
goodness," I said to Uncle Grady. "A very big family
must live here. They have gone out to play in the
middle of dinner."

"A squad of firefighters is like a family, Grover," Uncle Grady said. "They live and work together many hours a day. But they have not gone out to play. When the alarm sounds, firefighters have to stop whatever they are doing and race to the fire."

Then we went upstairs. "This is where we spend time
when we are not out fighting a fire," said Uncle Grady.
"When I am a firefighter, I will sleep here, too," I said.
"I hope I can bring my Teddy Monster."

"I will show you how firefighters get down to the garage when the alarm goes off in the middle of the night. We jump out of our beds and into our gear. Then we slide down this pole, right through a hole in the floor."

Wow! It was a long way down.

"Come on!" Uncle Grady said. "The fire trucks are coming back."

"1 ... 2 ... 3 fire trucks!" I counted as the trucks backed into the firehouse.

"Each truck does a different job," Uncle Grady explained.

40

41

"The rushing water from the pumper truck makes the fire hose jump around," said Uncle Grady. "That is why it takes more than one firefighter to handle each hose."

"I, Grover, would be a terrific hose handler," I told Uncle Grady. "I always help Mommy water our garden."

My favorite truck was the hook and ladder truck. Uncle Grady said the ladders can reach the windows of tall buildings.

There was a steering wheel in the front of the truck and another one in the back.

"The driver steers the front of the truck. The tiller is the driver who steers the back. That is how we get the hook and ladder truck around corners," said Uncle Grady.

"When I am a firefighter, can we drive a hook and ladder truck together?" I asked him. He liked that idea.

The firefighters were very busy. Some of them were
washing the fire trucks. Others were checking the
hoses for breaks.

"That looks like fun!" I told Uncle Grady.

"It is hard work," he said. "Firefighters have to be
sure their equipment is always ready to go."

When we got home, I told Mommy, "I want to put out fires, and steer a hook and ladder truck, and give baths to fire trucks, and help handle fire hoses.

"When I grow up, I want to be a firefighter."

I Want to Be A Doctor

By Liza Alexander
Illustrated by Lauren Attinello

One day I went to visit Granny Bird. She gave me a big
hug and a kiss on the beak. But something awful hap-
pened when Granny went up the stairs with my suitcase.
Just as she got to the top, she tripped and fell—THUNK!
  "Granny! Are you all right?" I asked.
  "Yes, dear," she said, "but I've hurt my ankle. Be a good
bird and run next door and see if Dr. Fuzzle is home."
  "Don't worry, Granny!" I said. "I'll be right back!"

KNOCK, KNOCK! I pounded on the Fuzzles' door. One of the little Fuzzles and his mommy opened it.

"Is the doctor in?" I asked.

"Yes," said the mommy, "I'm the doctor. You must be Mrs. Bird's grandson."

"That's right," I said. "How did you know?"

Then I told her all about Granny's fall, and she asked me to wait a minute while she got her bag.

As we walked back to Granny's I asked Dr. Fuzzle,
"What's inside your black bag?"

"My medical instruments," she answered.

So I said, "You mean like a violin and a piano?"

Dr. Fuzzle laughed and said, "No, different kinds of
instruments—tools that doctors use. You'll see what's
inside the bag when I examine your granny."

"Examine? What does that mean?" I asked.

"Examine means to look closely," the doctor told me. "When I examine your granny's ankle, I will feel it and try to understand what's wrong."

Granny was sitting in the same spot at the top of the stairs.

"Now, let's see, Mrs. Bird," said Dr. Fuzzle. "Yes. Your ankle is swollen. Does it hurt a lot or just a little?"

"It hurts a lot," said Granny.

Dr. Fuzzle moved Granny's foot gently from side to side. Then she said, "Tell me if this is painful."

"Ouch," said Granny. "That hurts."

Next Dr. Fuzzle asked me to help Granny to bed.
Granny leaned on us like we were crutches and
hopped on her one good leg to her room.

I smoothed Granny's blanket and plumped her pillows. "Thank you, dear," she said, and I felt good because I was taking care of Granny!

The doctor told us she thought that Granny's ankle was probably sprained, not broken. Then Dr. Fuzzle let me help wrap Granny's ankle in a bandage.

When we finished the bandaging, the doctor told Granny to put ice on her ankle and to keep her leg up. Dr. Fuzzle also told us to come to her office the next day so Granny's ankle could be X-rayed. Then Dr. Fuzzle said goodnight and went home.

Granny stayed in bed, so I brought our dinner up to
her room on a tray.
Then I washed the dishes all by myself!

I went upstairs and made sure Granny was okay.
Then I tucked her in and gave her a kiss goodnight
and went to bed myself. Boy, oh, boy, was I tired!

The next morning I was quite the early bird! I brought Granny breakfast in bed. She said it was delicious. I felt proud!

Then Granny asked me to find a cane in the back of her closet. Next I helped her get dressed.

We were ready to go. Granny told me to call a taxi, and we were off to Dr. Fuzzle's office.

Dr. Fuzzle took us straight to the X-ray room. She told us, "The X-ray machine is actually a big camera. We'll use it to take a picture of the bones inside your leg, Mrs. Bird."

Then the doctor lowered the big X-ray machine and switched it on and off—CLICK.

Then I asked the doctor, "Are you going to *examine* Granny now?"
"That's right, Big Bird," she said. "While we wait for the X-rays to develop, I'll give you a quick checkup, Mrs. Bird. All right?"
"Fine and dandy," said Granny.

63

The doctor was wearing a funny-looking necktie. She plugged it into her ears and held the bottom against Granny's chest. "What's that?" I asked.

"It's a stethoscope," said Dr. Fuzzle.

So I said it, too, "STETH-O-SCOPE." Then the doctor gave it to me so I could listen to Granny's heart, also. Her heart went *kathump-kathump-kathump*, and it was loud!

Then the doctor held an ice-cream-stick thing called a tongue depressor on Granny's tongue. She looked down Granny's throat with a tiny flashlight.

"Very fine!" said the doctor.

"And this is an otoscope," said Dr. Fuzzle. "It helps me
see that the passages inside your ear are clear, Mrs. Bird."
"Glad to *hear* it," said Granny, and we all laughed.

After that the doctor wrapped a cuff around Granny's
wing and squeezed a little bulb. The cuff filled up with air
like a water wing. "I am measuring your blood pressure."
"How is it?" asked Granny.
"Your blood pressure is just right," answered the doctor.
"Way to go, Granny!" I said.

Then a nurse came in and showed us the X-ray of Granny's ankle bones!

"Just as I thought," said Dr. Fuzzle. "No broken bones. Still, Mrs. Bird, stay off your feet as much as possible in the next few days so the sprain can heal. I'll give you some crutches so your ankle won't hurt so much."

"Dr. Fuzzle," I said, "I want to take X-ray pictures and carry a black bag with instruments in it. I want to listen to hearts with a stethoscope and examine people and birds and monsters. I want to be just like you!"

"Actually, Big Bird, you're already a lot like me," said Dr. Fuzzle. "Doctors help sick people and are curious about how bodies work."

Then Dr. Fuzzle showed me her medical school diploma. That's where she learned how to be a doctor. The diploma was framed on the wall and had a gold seal like a first prize! Soon it was time to go. Granny and I said, "So long!"

When we got home, Granny said, "I have an early birthday present for you, dear."

It was a black doctor's bag like Dr. Fuzzle's. Inside were toy medical instruments!

"Thank you for taking such good care of me," said Granny.

"I like taking care of you, Granny," I said. "And I need the practice. Because when I grow up, I want to be a doctor!"

I Want to Be
A Ballet Dancer

By Liza Alexander
Illustrated by Carol Nicklaus

Hello! My name is Prairie Dawn. Every Tuesday and
Thursday I take ballet class. I come to the studio early so
I can see the end of the class for the big boys and girls.
   I love to watch the big girls put on their toe shoes. The
toe shoes have satiny ribbons. The big girls look so pretty
when they glide across the floor on their tippy toes!

We change clothes in the dressing room. I wear a leotard and tights and tie my hair back off my face, just like the big girls do. I have little pink ballet slippers, but I am still too small to dance in toe shoes. I must wait until I am eleven or twelve and my bones and muscles are stronger.

It is time for our class to begin. First we warm up at
the barre. The barre is a pole attached along the wall.
We hold on to it to keep our balance.

We start each class with pliés. We look in the mirrors
to check that we are doing our best. A piano player plays
for us. We must listen very carefully so we can dance in
time to the music.

After our warm-up at the barre, we go to the middle of the floor. We practice the five positions of the feet and arms:

first position ...

second position ...

third ...

fourth ...

and fifth!

Sometimes we learn new steps. Today we are trying pirouettes. A pirouette is a twirl. We can't do pirouettes very well yet, but Miss Natalia says, "Practice makes perfect pirouettes!"

We are also working on little jumps
called changements. Here I go....

See! I am quite good at changements.

Now comes my favorite part of ballet class—big leaps!
We run, jump, stretch our legs out in a split, and soar
through the air like birds.

At the end of class we do our reverence.
Reverence is a fancy curtsy, which we do
to thank the piano player, our teacher,
and ourselves.

I am very happy! Miss Natalia has asked me to help
with the little kids' class. I will be a good helper. I took
the class when I was little, and I remember everything.

The tiny dancers do not use the barre. They are too small. They sit in a circle on the floor instead. We teach them the five positions and how to count to the music.

Miss Natalia is always saying, "Children! Pull in your tummies!" Or "Children, keep your backs straight! Pretend there is a glass of water on top of your head, and try not to spill it!"

At the end of the class we ask the tiny dancers to twirl
like snowflakes and hop like bunny rabbits!

Herry and I go to a performance of the Sesame Street Ballet. Miss Natalia gave me tickets to thank me for helping her. Miss Natalia herself is dancing! She is a member of the ballet company.

The ballet is perfectly beautiful! It tells a story in music and dance instead of words.

After the ballet we go backstage. Miss Natalia looks very happy but tired. The dancers make ballet look easy, but we dancers know that ballet can be hard work!

Herry wants to know if he can be a ballet dancer someday.

Miss Natalia smiles and says, "Just maybe, Herry,
if you keep taking classes and work hard. But you'll
have to study ballet for many years. Only the very best
dancers can become members of ballet companies."

Then Miss Natalia unties her toe shoes and takes them off. She signs her name twice, right on the toes, and gives the toe shoes to me to keep! This is the most exciting moment of my life ... because when I grow up, I want to be a ballet dancer.

I Want to Be
A Veterinarian

By Michaela Muntean
Illustrated by Tom Cooke

Today I had to take Barkley to the doctor. Barkley wasn't
sick. It was time for his yearly checkup. Animals need to
have checkups just like people. Doctors who take care of
animals have a special name. They are called veterinarians.
I like to visit the veterinarian with Barkley.

When we arrived, there was a girl with a new puppy waiting to see Dr. Duberman.

"What's your puppy's name?" I asked.

"Woofer," said the girl. I said hello to Woofer, and Barkley said hello, too.

"Woof," said Barkley.

"Woof," answered Woofer.

I remember when Barkley was a puppy. The doctor told me how to take care of him. He told me how to bathe Barkley and brush him. He told me what to feed him and how to train him. Teaching people how to take good care of their pets is part of a veterinarian's job.

The doctor called Woofer's name, and he and the girl
went into the examining room. While we were waiting,
other people and their pets arrived. Some of the animals
hadn't come just for a checkup. There was a bird with a
hurt wing. There was a cat with a cast on one leg.

The doctor called Barkley's name, and it was our turn to
go into the examining room. Barkley wasn't worried. He'd
been there before, and Dr. Duberman was kind and gentle.

"Hello, Barkley," said Dr. Duberman as he patted Barkley on the head. "You seem to be just fine, but I want to have a closer look at you."

The veterinarian listened to Barkley's heartbeat with a stethoscope.

He looked in Barkley's eyes and ears with a little flashlight.

He checked his teeth to make sure they were clean and strong. A veterinarian is also an animal's dentist.

The doctor weighed Barkley on a big scale. Then he checked Barkley's paws and looked at his fur and skin. "Good," said Dr. Duberman. "No fleas." Next he gave Barkley his yearly shot. It only hurt for a minute.

When the doctor was finished, he said, "That's all for today. A fine checkup for a fine, healthy dog."

Barkley said, "Woof," and I said, "Good-bye, Doctor. Thank you." Then Barkley and I were on our way.

Maybe someday I will be a veterinarian like Dr. Duberman and take care of animals. I know you have to go to school and study very hard. There are lots of things you have to learn to be a veterinarian.

After I graduate from school, I will have an office just like Dr. Duberman's. It will have an X-ray machine so I can see if an animal has any broken bones.

I will carry a flashlight, and I will wear a stethoscope
around my neck. When animals are sick, I will give
them medicine to make them well.

I will take care of all kinds of pets—cats and dogs and
bunnies and turtles and guinea pigs and even goldfish.

Some veterinarians take care of farm animals. Maybe that's what I will do! Then I will have to visit my patients on the farm, because it is very hard to bring a cow or a goat to an office.

Veterinarians make sure that chickens stay healthy so they
will lay lots of eggs. They take care of dairy cows so the cows
will produce good milk.

Sometimes veterinarians help to deliver the foal when a mother horse is having a baby.

Some veterinarians take care of zoo animals.
Maybe that's what I'll do. I wonder how I would
take care of an elephant with an earache!

Or a giraffe with a sore throat!

Someday I will learn how to take care of all kinds
of animals, whether they have fur or fins or feathers,
paws or claws or hooves, because when I grow up...

I want to be a veterinarian!

I Want to Be A Teacher

By Michaela Muntean
Illustrated by David Prebenna

I like school. I like my classroom and my desk. I like my teacher, Mr. Redman, too. Someday I am going to be just like him.

To be a good teacher you have to know a lot of things. You have to know the alphabet, and you have to be a good reader. You have to know all about numbers and colors and shapes, and you have to know lots of songs and stories.

1 2 3 4

Sometimes Ernie and I play school at home. We set up our desks and chalkboard in the living room. We pretend it's a classroom.

One rainy day we decided to play school. I put the chalkboard next to my desk because I was going to pretend to be Mr. Redman. Everything was ready, but Ernie wasn't sitting at his desk. He was in the kitchen.

"What are you doing?" I called to him.

"I'm packing my lunch," Ernie answered.

"Hurry up!" I said. "It's time for school to start."

"Gee, Bert," Ernie said when he finally finished,
"where is my cubby for my stuff?"
   We didn't have a real cubby, so we decided that
Ernie should put his lunch box in the closet.

I said, "Good morning, class," just like Mr. Redman does. "Today we are going to learn about weather."

Ernie raised his hand. "I want to know whether or not it will keep raining all day," he said. "Hee-hee-hee. Do you get it, Bert? *Whether* it will rain..."

"Yes, Ernie, I get it," I said. "Now please pay attention."

So I started to teach. I wrote the word SNOW on the chalkboard. I told Ernie that no two snowflakes are alike. Each one has its own special pattern.

For art time we cut snowflakes out of white paper and hung them up.

"Gee, Bert," said Ernie, "this is fun. And look. No two are alike!"

Then I wrote the word WIND on the chalkboard.
We turned on the fan and pretended it was the wind
blowing our snowflakes.

132

Next I wrote the word RAIN. We could see what rain was like by looking out the window. So we practiced our numbers by counting the raindrops on the windowpane. We counted twenty-four.

At music time we sang "The Itsy-Bitsy Spider"
because it was the only song I knew that had rain in it.
It goes like this:

The itsy-bitsy spider climbed up the water spout.
Down came the rain and washed the spider out.
Out came the sun and dried up all the rain,
And the itsy-bitsy spider climbed up the spout again.

For story time I read *The Brave Little Pigeon* to Ernie.
It is a story about a pigeon named Puffy. Puffy has to
fly through a terrible snowstorm to deliver an important
message. The message saves everyone in the town, and
Puffy is a hero. It is one of my favorite stories.

After story time, we had quiet time. Ernie got his
blanket and spread it out on the floor. While he rested,
I sharpened pencils and straightened up my desk.

When quiet time was over, I wrote the words SPRING, SUMMER, FALL, and WINTER on the chalkboard. We talked about the different kinds of weather in each season.

I asked Ernie to draw a picture of a tree in each season. He drew one tree with a few little leaves, one tree with lots of green leaves, one tree with red and yellow leaves, and one tree with snow on the branches. It was a good picture. I told Ernie I liked it.

Then I taught Ernie a poem. Uncle Bart taught it to me, and this is how it goes:

Oh, trees, you are so silly.
You wear a lot when it's hot
And nothing when it's chilly!

Ernie liked the poem and said it five times so he wouldn't forget it.

"For alphabet time we are going to play a word game," I said.
"What letter does the word WINDOW start with?"

"W," said Ernie. "WINDOW starts with the letter W. If you
look out the WINDOW, Bert, you'll see that it has stopped
raining and the sun is shining. Is it time for lunch? We could
eat in the park. I packed a sandwich for you, too."

I wanted to go on teaching, but I was hungry, too. So I said, "School is over for today. Let's go outside and enjoy the weather."

Ernie ran to get his lunch box. Then he raised his hand.

"Do you have a question?" I asked. I sounded just like Mr. Redman.

"No, I have something to say," said Ernie.
"What is it, Ernie?" I asked.
"I just want to say that you are really good at teaching, old buddy. I learned a lot today!"
I smiled. "Oh, I am so glad," I said. "Because when I grow up, I want to be a teacher!"